k	H
r	K
e	R
h	M
m	E
c	D
d	C

Adam has a pet stick insect.

a stick insect

a stick

Het has a pet kitten.

Het's kitten is a pest.
□ a rip
□ a crack
□ mess

Stick insect sat in its tank.

Kitten crept in.
Hiss!

Stick insect hid in Adam's desk.

Tip!

Het's kitten is trapped!

Dad!
Adam panics.

Dad steps in.
A-ha!